Howling Nightmares

Terrifying Tales of Horror and Terror

Table of Contents

Introduction
Chapter 1: The Haunted House on Hollow Hill
Chapter 2: The Abandoned Asylums Dark Secret
Chapter 3: The Ghost of Blackwood Manor
Chapter 4: The Curse of the Crying Woman
Chapter 5: The Demon Within the Doll
Chapter 6: The Terror in the Tunnels
Chapter 7: The Blood Moon Ritual
Chapter 8: The Lake of Lost Souls
Chapter 9: The Phantom Hitchhiker
Chapter 10: The Witching Hour at Willow Creek
Chapter 11: The Shadow in the Attic
Chapter 12: The Monster in the Mirror

Chapter 13: The Last Will and Testament of Thomas Smith

Chapter 14: The Secret of the Sealed Room

Chapter 15: The Devil's Playground

Chapter 16: The Dollmaker's Deadly Creations

Chapter 17: The Mysterious Disappearance of Sarah Thomas

Chapter 18: The Dark Harvest Festival

Chapter 19: The House That Time Forgot

Chapter 20: The Night the Dead Came to Life

Chapter 21: The Vengeful Ghost of Emily James

Chapter 22: The Island of the Damned

Chapter 23: The Midnight Caller

Chapter 24: The Legend of the Bloody Bride

Chapter 25: The Cursed Forest of Lost Souls

Chapter 26: The Scream Queen's Revenge

Chapter 27: The Witch of Whispering Woods

Chapter 28: The Killer in the Cornfield

Chapter 29: The Specter of Stonehurst Cemetery

Chapter 30: The House of Horrors

Chapter 31: The Dollhouse Murders

Chapter 32: The Curse of the Black Cat

Chapter 33: The Ghostly Guardian of Glenwood Manor

Chapter 34: The Bloodstained Bride

Chapter 35: The Demon's Den

Chapter 36: The Children of the Corn Stalks

Chapter 37: The Midnight Curse of Moonlight Manor

Chapter 38: The Possession of Mary Brown
Chapter 39: The Whispering Woman of the Windmill
Chapter 40: The Haunted Hotel on the Hill
Chapter 41: The Soul Eater's Sanctuary
Chapter 42: The Shadowy Stranger on the Subway
Chapter 43: The Chanting Cult of Candlewood Creek
Chapter 44: The Butcher of Briarwood Farm
Chapter 45: The Lost City of the Dead
Chapter 46: The Phantom of the Opera House
Chapter 47: The Grinning Ghost of Greenwood Cemetery
Chapter 48: The Killer in the Mirror Maze
Chapter 49: The House of the Headless Horseman
Chapter 50: The Secret Society of the Sorcerers

Conclusion

Introduction

Welcome to "Howling Nightmares: Terrifying Tales of Horror and Terror". This collection of 50 horror stories will take you on a journey through the darkest corners of the human imagination and beyond. From haunted houses and abandoned asylums to cursed forests and demonic dolls, these stories will leave you on the edge of your seat, afraid to turn the page yet unable to look away.

Each story is a unique and gripping tale of horror, carefully crafted to keep you guessing until the very end. You'll meet characters who are driven to the brink of madness by the horrors they encounter, and witness unspeakable acts of violence and depravity that will chill you to the bone. But amidst the darkness and despair, there are also glimmers of hope and redemption, as some characters find the strength to confront their fears and fight back against the evil that threatens to consume them.

Whether you're a fan of classic horror tropes or prefer more modern twists on the genre, "Howling Nightmares" has something for everyone. So settle in, turn off the lights, and prepare to be scared. These stories will haunt you long after you've turned the final page.

Chapter 1

The Haunted House on Hollow Hill

It was a dark and stormy night when Sarah and her friends decided to explore the old mansion on Hollow Hill. They had heard rumors of strange occurrences and unexplainable noises coming from the abandoned house, but they were determined to uncover the truth.

As they approached the house, the wind howled through the trees and the rain lashed down upon them.

The front door creaked open as they pushed it aside, revealing a dimly lit hallway filled with cobwebs and dust.

The group moved cautiously through the house, their flashlights illuminating the peeling wallpaper and broken furniture. They heard whispers and footsteps coming from the empty rooms, but every time they turned to investigate, there was nothing there.

As they reached the top of the staircase, Sarah felt a cold breeze brush against her neck. She turned to see a figure standing at the end of the hallway, its eyes glowing in the darkness.

Trembling with fear, the group backed away as the figure moved closer, its presence filling the room with a sense of dread. Suddenly, the walls began to shake and the floor opened up beneath them, sending them tumbling into the depths below.

When they finally emerged from the rubble, they found themselves in a room filled with twisted and decaying corpses. The figure from the hallway stood before them, its face twisted into a grotesque grin.

Sarah and her friends screamed in terror as the figure reached out to claim them, and they knew they had uncovered something far more sinister than they had ever imagined. They had awakened an ancient evil, and it would never let them leave the haunted house on Hollow Hill alive.

Chapter 2

The Abandoned Asylums Dark Secret

The abandoned asylum on the outskirts of town had always been a source of curiosity for John. He had heard stories of the brutal treatments that had been administered to the patients there and was fascinated by the idea of exploring the decaying building.

One day, John decided to finally explore the asylum, despite the warnings of his friends. As he walked through the deserted halls, he felt a sense of unease settle over him. The air was thick with the stench of decay, and the only sound was the soft shuffling of his footsteps.

As he turned a corner, he saw a door hanging off its hinges. Inside, he found a room filled with old medical equipment and restraints. The sight made him shudder, and he quickly left the room.

But as he continued through the asylum, he heard strange whispers and footsteps behind him. Every time he turned around, there was nothing there. He could feel a presence following him, lurking in the shadows just out of sight.

Finally, John came to a door that was locked from the outside. He knew that he had to see what was inside, so he used a crowbar to break the lock.

Inside, he found a room filled with old journals and case files. As he read through them, he realized the terrible truth of the asylum's dark past. The doctors had been performing twisted experiments on the patients, trying to unlock the secrets of the human mind. But their methods were cruel and inhumane, and many of the patients had died as a result.

Suddenly, John heard a sound behind him. He turned to see a figure standing in the doorway, its eyes glowing with malevolent energy. It was one of the patients, its mind twisted by the horrors that had been inflicted upon it.

John knew that he had to escape the asylum before the patient could catch him, but as he turned to run, he found the door had been locked from the outside. He was trapped, with only the horrors of the abandoned asylum and its dark secrets for company.

Chapter 3

The Ghost of Blackwood Manor

Sophie had always been fascinated by the stories of the ghost of Blackwood Manor. The sprawling estate had been abandoned for decades, and locals whispered that the ghost of the former owner still haunted its halls.

One day, Sophie decided to explore the mansion for herself. She climbed over the rusted gates and made her way through the overgrown gardens until she reached the front door.

As she stepped into the foyer, she felt a chill run down her spine. The air was thick with the scent of decay and neglect, and she could hear faint whispers and laughter echoing through the halls.

Determined to find the source of the ghostly activity, Sophie began to search the house room by room. But the deeper she went, the more she felt like she was being watched.

In one of the upstairs bedrooms, Sophie saw a faint apparition standing in the corner. It was the ghost of a woman, dressed in a Victorian-era gown, with a haunted look in her eyes.

Sophie tried to speak to the ghost, but it simply stared back at her, its face frozen in a sad expression. Suddenly, the room grew cold and Sophie could feel a presence moving closer to her.

She turned around to see a figure looming in the doorway, its face twisted in a grotesque snarl. Sophie screamed and ran, the ghostly presence hot on her heels.

As she burst out of the mansion and into the bright sunshine, she knew she would never forget the terror she had experienced in Blackwood Manor. She had come face to face with the ghost of the former owner, and it was not a pleasant encounter.

Chapter 4

The Curse of the Crying Woman

When Maria moved into her new home on the outskirts of town, she didn't expect to be haunted by the ghost of a weeping woman. Every night, Maria heard the sound of mournful sobbing coming from the walls, and no matter how hard she tried, she couldn't escape the haunting cries.

Determined to uncover the truth, Maria delved into the history of her new home, and what she discovered left her trembling with fear. The previous owners had been involved in a tragic accident that had claimed the life of their daughter, and the grieving mother had cursed the house with her tears.

Maria knew she had to break the curse if she ever wanted to find peace in her home, but she didn't know how. That is until she met an old woman in the park, who told her of a magical charm that could banish the weeping woman forever.

Maria followed the old woman's instructions and soon found herself standing in front of the cursed house, clutching the charm in her hand. As she recited the incantation, the house shook and the sound of wailing filled the air.

But when the noise subsided, Maria realized she had made a grave mistake. The curse was not lifted, but instead had transferred to her. She was now the one haunted by the ghost of the weeping woman, cursed to carry the burden of her grief for all eternity.

Desperate to break free from the curse, Maria tried everything she could think of, but nothing worked. She was doomed to spend the rest of her days as the crying woman, a ghostly figure haunting the very home she had hoped to escape.

And so the legend of the crying woman lived on, a warning to all those who dared to enter the cursed house and awaken the wrath of a grieving mother.

Chapter 5

The Demon Within the Doll

When Maggie inherited her grandmother's antique doll collection, she was thrilled. She had always loved dolls and couldn't wait to add them to her own collection. But there was one doll in particular that caught her eye. It was an old porcelain doll with black hair and glassy eyes that seemed to follow her wherever she went.

As Maggie began to display the dolls in her room, she noticed that strange things started happening. The temperature would drop suddenly, and she would hear whispers and footsteps in the hallway at night. But the strangest thing was that the dolls seemed to move on their own, as if they had a life of their own.

One night, as Maggie was getting ready for bed, she noticed that the porcelain doll had moved from its shelf and was now sitting on her dresser. But as she approached the doll, she realized that something was horribly wrong. Its eyes were no longer glassy, but instead, they were glowing red.

Suddenly, the doll sprang to life and leapt at Maggie, its mouth open wide in a silent scream. Maggie stumbled backwards and fell to the floor, screaming for help. But no one came, and the doll continued to advance.

It wasn't until Maggie remembered the ritual her grandmother had told her about that she realized what she had to do. She had to destroy the doll before it destroyed her. Maggie quickly gathered the materials she needed and performed the ritual, hoping against hope that it would work.

As the final words left her lips, the porcelain doll shattered into a million pieces, and the room was filled with a blinding light. When Maggie opened her eyes, she was alone in her room, and the other dolls were once again in their proper places.

But as Maggie looked at the shattered pieces of the porcelain doll, she realized that something was still wrong. The demon that had possessed the doll was still out there, and it was only a matter of time before it found a new host.

Chapter 6

The Terror in the Tunnels

For years, the abandoned subway tunnels beneath the city had been a popular spot for urban explorers and thrill-seekers. But when a group of friends decided to venture into the depths of the tunnels one night, they quickly realized they had made a grave mistake.

As they descended deeper into the maze of tunnels, they heard strange noises echoing through the darkness. At first, they thought it was just the sound of rats scurrying along the tracks, but soon they realized it was something much more sinister.

The group heard the sound of heavy breathing and footsteps getting closer and closer. They could see the outline of a figure moving towards them, its eyes glowing in the darkness.

Panic set in as the group tried to run, but the tunnels seemed to twist and turn in impossible ways, trapping them in a never-ending maze. They could hear the figure getting closer, its breath hot on their necks.

Finally, they came to a dead end, and the figure stood before them, its face twisted into a grotesque mask of terror. It was a creature unlike anything they had ever seen, with razor-sharp claws and glowing red eyes that seemed to peer into their very souls.

The creature attacked with a ferocity that left the group no chance of escape. One by one, they fell to its claws, their screams echoing through the tunnels until the only sound left was the creature's triumphant roar.

When the police finally found the bodies, they could hardly believe the gruesome scene before them. The tunnels were sealed off, and the legend of the terror in the tunnels was born, a cautionary tale for anyone foolish enough to venture into the darkness alone.

Chapter 7

The Blood Moon Ritual

It was the night of the blood moon, and a group of teenagers had gathered in the woods to perform an ancient ritual. They had heard rumors of a powerful force that could be summoned during the lunar eclipse, and they were eager to try their luck.

As the moon turned red and the sky grew dark, the group lit candles and drew a circle in the dirt. They recited an incantation that they had found in an old book, and soon they felt a strange energy pulsing through the air.

Suddenly, the ground began to shake, and a figure emerged from the shadows. It was a tall, hooded figure with eyes that glowed like hot coals. The teenagers felt a sense of both awe and terror as the figure spoke to them in a language they could not understand.

Without warning, the figure began to draw symbols in the dirt around the circle. The teenagers watched in horror as the symbols began to glow, and they realized that they had summoned something far beyond their control.

The figure spoke again, and this time its words were clear. "I demand a sacrifice," it said, its voice echoing through the woods.

The teenagers looked at each other in horror, realizing too late the terrible mistake they had made. They were trapped, with no escape from the figure's demands.

As the blood moon reached its peak, the figure began to chant, and the teenagers felt a force pulling at their bodies. They screamed in pain and terror as their blood was drained from their bodies, fueling the dark power that the figure had summoned.

When it was over, there was nothing left but empty husks of flesh. The figure vanished into the darkness, leaving behind only a circle of blood and a memory that would haunt the few who survived for the rest of their lives. They had played with forces they could not comprehend, and they had paid the ultimate price.

Chapter 8

The Lake of Lost Souls

For generations, the locals had whispered about the lake that lay deep in the heart of the forest. They spoke of strange happenings and disappearances, warning their children to stay far away.

But for Jake and his friends, the tales of the lake only piqued their curiosity. They decided to investigate, convinced that the rumors were nothing more than superstition.

As they approached the shore of the lake, they felt an eerie silence descend upon the forest. The water was still and dark, reflecting the trees like a mirror. But as they gazed into the depths, they saw movement beneath the surface. Shapes that writhed and twisted like snakes.

Suddenly, a hand reached out of the water and dragged one of Jake's friends under. The others screamed in terror and tried to pull him back, but it was too late. He was gone.

The water began to churn and bubble, and more hands emerged from the depths, pulling the other friends down one by one. Jake struggled to keep his head above water, but the hands grasped at him, pulling him closer to the bottom of the lake.

As he sank into the cold, black depths, he saw the faces of the lost souls that had drowned in the lake over the years. They were twisted and contorted, their eyes filled with a hunger for revenge.

Jake realized too late that the lake was cursed, and that the lost souls had claimed him as their latest victim. He felt their hands dragging him down into the darkness, and he knew that he would never be seen again. The lake of lost souls had claimed another victim, and it would never give him up.

Chapter 9

The Phantom Hitchhiker

It was a warm summer evening when John decided to drive home from his friend's party. The road was dark and deserted, and he was feeling tired and a little bit drunk. Suddenly, he saw a figure standing at the side of the road, waving for him to stop.

John slowed down and rolled down his window, but the figure was obscured by the darkness. "Can I help you?" he asked.

The figure stepped closer, revealing a beautiful young woman with long, dark hair and piercing blue eyes. She told him that she had been in a car accident and needed a ride home.

John felt a pang of sympathy for the woman and agreed to give her a lift. She climbed into the passenger seat and directed him to a remote part of town.

As they drove, the woman grew increasingly silent and distant. John tried to make small talk, but she didn't seem interested. When they arrived at the address she had given him, she thanked him and disappeared into the darkness without a word of goodbye.

Confused and a little bit unnerved, John continued on his way home. But as he drove, he began to notice a strange sensation in the car. It was as if the air around him had grown thick and heavy, and he felt a sense of foreboding creeping up his spine.

Suddenly, he heard a faint whispering coming from the backseat. He turned around, but there was nobody there. The whispering grew louder and more insistent, and John realized that he was not alone in the car.

He felt a cold hand on his shoulder and turned to see the woman from before, her face twisted into a demonic mask of rage. She had been dead all along, and now she was seeking revenge on those who had caused her untimely demise.

John screamed in terror as the car careened off the road and into a ditch. He knew he would never escape the phantom hitchhiker's wrath, and his fate would be sealed forever.

Chapter 10

The Witching Hour at Willow Creek

As the clock struck midnight on Halloween night, a group of teenagers decided to explore the old witch's hut at Willow Creek. They had heard rumors of strange happenings and supernatural powers, but they didn't believe in such nonsense. They were just looking for a scare.

As they approached the hut, they saw flickering lights and heard eerie whispers coming from within. They pushed open the door and stepped inside, only to be met with a strange and unsettling silence.

Suddenly, a figure appeared before them, its face hidden behind a hooded cloak. The teens tried to run, but they found themselves trapped in a circle of stones that seemed to glow with an otherworldly energy.

The figure began to chant, its voice rising in pitch and intensity. The air grew thick with the smell of sulfur and the sound of cackling laughter echoed through the clearing.

One by one, the teens began to feel a strange sensation in their bodies, as if they were being pulled towards the center of the circle. They screamed in terror as their limbs contorted and twisted, their bodies convulsing with an unseen force.

When the chanting finally stopped, the teens lay motionless on the ground, their eyes glazed over with a strange, otherworldly glow. The figure removed its hood to reveal a withered and ancient face, its eyes filled with malice and power.

The teens had unknowingly stumbled into the witching hour at Willow Creek, and they had paid the ultimate price for their curiosity. From that night on, the witch's curse would haunt their dreams and their waking hours, a reminder of the dangers that lurked in the darkness beyond.

Chapter 11

The Shadow in the Attic

When Rachel inherited her grandfather's old house, she was thrilled at the prospect of finally having a place of her own. But as she settled in and began to explore the house, she couldn't shake the feeling that something was off.

One day, while rummaging through the clutter in the attic, Rachel noticed a strange shadow moving along the far wall. At first, she thought it was just her imagination playing tricks on her, but the more she stared, the more convinced she became that there was something in the room with her.

As she approached the shadow, she felt a chill run down her spine. The shadow seemed to be alive, twisting and turning in impossible ways. She tried to back away, but found herself frozen in place, unable to move.

Suddenly, the shadow lunged at her, enveloping her in darkness. Rachel felt as though she was being suffocated, her screams muffled by the void around her.

When she finally emerged from the shadow's grasp, she was shaken and disoriented. The attic was now completely empty, the shadow gone without a trace.

Rachel tried to put the incident out of her mind, but she couldn't escape the feeling that something was still watching her from the shadows. As the days passed, she began to experience strange occurrences throughout the house - doors opening and closing on their own, whispers in the darkness, and the feeling of being watched wherever she went.

Desperate to uncover the truth, Rachel returned to the attic and began to dig through her grandfather's belongings. It was then that she discovered an old diary, filled with entries about a shadow creature that had haunted her grandfather for years.

As she read through the pages, Rachel realized that the shadow had been passed down through her family for generations, and that it was now her turn to face its wrath.

With a sense of dread, Rachel knew that she would never be able to escape the shadow in the attic. It had claimed her family before her, and it would continue to haunt them for generations to come.

Chapter 12

The Monster in the Mirror

Samantha had always been afraid of mirrors. Ever since she was a child, she had felt like something was watching her from the other side, waiting to pounce. But she had learned to live with her fear, avoiding mirrors whenever possible and covering them up when she couldn't.

One day, Samantha was shopping at a thrift store when she saw an antique mirror that caught her eye. It was ornately carved and seemed to glow with an otherworldly light. Despite her fear, Samantha couldn't resist the mirror's allure, and she bought it on the spot.

When she got home, Samantha hung the mirror on her bedroom wall, convinced that its beauty would help her overcome her fear. But that night, as she lay in bed, she heard a soft whisper coming from the mirror. At first, she thought it was just her imagination, but then the whisper grew louder and more insistent.

Samantha approached the mirror cautiously, her heart pounding in her chest. As she peered into its depths, she saw a shadowy figure staring back at her, its eyes glowing with an eerie light.

Terrified, Samantha tried to look away, but the figure in the mirror held her gaze. Slowly, it reached out a hand, beckoning to her.

In a trance-like state, Samantha stepped closer to the mirror, her hand outstretched. Suddenly, the figure reached through the glass and grabbed her, pulling her into the mirror's realm.

Samantha found herself in a dark and twisted world, filled with monstrous creatures and twisted, nightmarish landscapes. She realized too late that the figure in the mirror was not a reflection, but a gateway to a realm of horror beyond her worst nightmares.

As Samantha tried to find a way out, she realized that the only way to escape was to confront the monster in the mirror and defeat it. With every step, the world grew darker and more dangerous, and Samantha knew that her only hope was to find the courage to face her deepest fears and destroy the monster once and for all.

Chapter 13

The Last Will and Testament of Thomas Smith

Thomas Smith was a wealthy man who had spent his entire life collecting rare and valuable antiques from around the world. As he lay on his deathbed, he knew that his time was running out, and he summoned his lawyer to read his last will and testament.

To the surprise of his family and friends, Thomas had left all of his possessions to a mysterious stranger named Lucinda, whom nobody had ever heard of before. His lawyer was instructed to deliver a letter to Lucinda, inviting her to claim her inheritance and to meet with Thomas's family and friends at his estate.

The letter stated that Lucinda was to arrive on the night of the full moon, and that she was to bring a single item of her choosing with her. The family and friends were instructed to gather in the drawing room, where Thomas's lawyer would read a second letter that would reveal the true purpose of Thomas's final wishes.

As the full moon rose over the estate, Lucinda arrived with a small, ornate box in her hands. The family and friends gathered in the drawing room, anxiously waiting for the lawyer to read the second letter.

The letter revealed that Thomas had made a deal with a demon many years ago, trading his soul in exchange for wealth and power. He had accumulated a vast collection of antiques over the years, each one imbued with dark magic and possessed by malevolent spirits.

Thomas's dying wish was for Lucinda to take possession of the cursed objects and to continue his legacy, summoning the spirits of the dead to do her bidding. In exchange, Thomas promised to release Lucinda from the deal with the demon, allowing her to live a life of wealth and power until the end of her days.

As the family and friends watched in horror, Lucinda opened the small box and revealed a small, silver dagger. With a wicked grin on her face, she plunged the dagger into her own chest, unleashing a torrent of dark energy that consumed the room.

Thomas's spirit appeared before them, his face twisted in rage and despair. He had been tricked by the demon, and now his legacy would continue on through Lucinda, forever bound to the cursed objects that he had amassed.

The family and friends fled the estate, knowing that they had witnessed something far more sinister than they could ever have imagined. They would never forget the last will and testament of Thomas Smith, and the dark magic that lurked within his collection of cursed antiques.

Chapter 14

The Secret of the Sealed Room

When the new owners of the old Victorian mansion discovered a room that had been sealed shut for years, they were both excited and curious to find out what secrets it held. The room was located on the top floor of the house and had no windows, making it dark and foreboding.

As they pried open the door, they were hit with a musty smell that seemed to cling to their skin. The room was filled with old furniture and boxes, covered in dust and cobwebs.

But as they began to sift through the items, they discovered a strange, leather-bound book that was unlike anything they had ever seen before. Its pages were filled with bizarre drawings and strange symbols, and the language it was written in was completely foreign to them.

The couple quickly became obsessed with deciphering the book's contents and spent long hours pouring over its pages. But as they delved deeper into its secrets, they began to notice strange things happening around them.

The temperature in the room would suddenly drop, and they could hear faint whispers and murmurs coming from the walls. Objects would move on their own, and they began to feel a sense of being watched.

One night, as they were studying the book, they heard a loud banging on the door. When they opened it, they found no one outside, but the book had vanished from the table.

Determined to find it, they searched the house from top to bottom, but it was nowhere to be found. That's when they realized that the book was more than just a simple artifact. It was a gateway to something far more sinister, something that had been waiting for centuries to be unleashed.

As they frantically searched for a way to stop the evil they had unleashed, they realized that they were in way over their heads. They had awakened something they could not control, and it was only a matter of time before it consumed them all.

Chapter 15

The Devil's Playground

Tara had always been fascinated by abandoned amusement parks, and she couldn't resist the opportunity to explore the long-forgotten park that lay at the edge of town. She had heard rumors of strange sightings and unexplained disappearances in the park, but she brushed them off as mere urban legends.

As she stepped through the rusted gates, however, Tara felt a chill run down her spine. The park was eerily quiet, the rides still and silent in the darkness.

Tara began to explore, walking past the dilapidated roller coaster and the crumbling carousel. She paused at the funhouse, its twisted mirrors reflecting a distorted version of herself. As she turned to leave, she heard a faint whisper in her ear, "Welcome to the Devil's Playground."

Tara spun around, but there was no one there. She shook her head and continued on, but the whispering continued to follow her. She tried to ignore it, but it grew louder and more insistent with each step.

Suddenly, the ground beneath her feet gave way, and Tara tumbled into a dark underground chamber. As she struggled to get her bearings, she realized that she was not alone. The chamber was filled with grotesque, demon-like creatures, their eyes glowing in the darkness.

Tara screamed in terror as the creatures closed in on her, their claws and teeth gleaming in the dim light. She ran, but there was nowhere to hide in the claustrophobic space. She was trapped in the Devil's Playground, with no hope of escape.

As the demons closed in on her, Tara realized the true horror of what she had stumbled upon. The abandoned amusement park was not just a forgotten relic of the past. It was a portal to hell, a playground for the devil and his minions.

Tara knew then that she would never leave the Devil's Playground alive, but she would not go down without a fight. With a fierce determination, she turned to face her attackers, ready to take on the demons of the underworld.

Chapter 16

The Dollmaker's Deadly Creations

Lila always loved dolls, so when she stumbled upon a quaint little shop run by an old man called the Dollmaker, she was thrilled. The Dollmaker's dolls were unlike any Lila had ever seen before - each one was exquisitely crafted with lifelike features and intricate details.

Lila couldn't resist buying one of the dolls, and she quickly grew attached to it. She named it Bella and brought it with her wherever she went. But soon, strange things began to happen.

Lila would wake up in the middle of the night to find Bella staring at her with an unnerving expression. And whenever she left the room, she swore she could hear the sound of tiny footsteps following her.

As the days went on, the dolls in the shop seemed to multiply, each one more sinister than the last. Lila tried to ignore the feeling of dread that was growing within her, but she couldn't shake the feeling that something was terribly wrong.

One night, she decided to go back to the Dollmaker's shop to confront him about the strange occurrences. When she arrived, she found the shop filled with dolls, all of them staring at her with their dead eyes.

Suddenly, the Dollmaker appeared, his twisted smile sending chills down Lila's spine. He revealed that he had been using dark magic to bring his dolls to life, and that they were now under his control.

As Lila tried to escape, she found herself surrounded by the dolls, their cold fingers reaching out to claim her. But just as she thought all was lost, she remembered a spell her grandmother had taught her for banishing evil spirits.

With a trembling voice, Lila spoke the incantation, and the dolls were sucked back into their lifeless forms. The Dollmaker screamed in rage, but Lila managed to escape, vowing to never return to that cursed shop again.

But as she walked away, she couldn't help but feel that the Dollmaker's dark magic was still out there, waiting to claim its next victim.

Chapter 17

The Mysterious Disappearance of Sarah Thomas

Sarah Thomas was a young woman with a passion for exploring abandoned places. She had heard rumors of an old factory on the outskirts of town that had been closed down for years, and she couldn't resist the temptation to investigate.

As she made her way through the rusted gates and into the factory, Sarah felt a sense of excitement and anticipation. The air was thick with the scent of oil and metal, and the sound of machinery echoed through the empty corridors.

As she explored the maze of rooms and corridors, Sarah heard whispers and footsteps coming from the darkness. She called out, but there was no answer. Suddenly, the lights flickered and went out, leaving her in complete darkness.

Panic rising within her, Sarah fumbled for her flashlight, but it wouldn't turn on. She tried to retrace her steps, but the layout of the factory had become a confusing labyrinth. Suddenly, she heard a voice whisper her name. It was a voice she recognized, but it was distorted, as if coming from a great distance.

Sarah followed the voice through the darkened factory, her heart pounding in her chest. The voice led her to a room at the end of a long hallway, where she saw a figure standing in the shadows.

The figure stepped forward, revealing itself to be a twisted and distorted version of Sarah herself. It spoke to her in a raspy, unnatural voice, telling her that she had stumbled upon a portal to another dimension.

In terror, Sarah tried to flee, but the distorted figure grabbed hold of her, dragging her towards the portal. Sarah struggled to break free, but the figure was too strong.

The last thing Sarah remembered was being pulled into the portal, her screams echoing through the empty factory. When the authorities arrived, they found no trace of her, and the factory was sealed off for good.

To this day, no one knows what happened to Sarah Thomas or what lies beyond the portal in that abandoned factory. But those who venture too close to the sealed gates can still hear her voice calling out from the darkness, warning them to stay away.

Chapter 18

The Dark Harvest Festival

For years, the small town of Millfield had held an annual harvest festival to celebrate the bounty of the season. But this year was different. As the townsfolk prepared for the festival, a sinister energy seemed to permeate the air, and rumors of strange happenings began to circulate.

On the night of the festival, a group of teenagers decided to sneak into the abandoned barn on the outskirts of town. They had heard that something dark and sinister was happening there, and they were determined to uncover the truth.

As they entered the barn, they found themselves surrounded by a strange, almost palpable darkness. The air was thick with the scent of rotting vegetation and the low hum of chanting filled their ears.

Suddenly, the chanting stopped and the barn was filled with an eerie silence. The teenagers looked up to see a group of cloaked figures standing before them, their faces obscured by shadow.

The figures began to move in a slow, synchronized dance, their movements becoming more frenzied with each passing moment. The air grew hotter and thicker, and the teenagers began to feel dizzy and disoriented.

Just as they thought they couldn't take it any longer, the figures stopped moving and the darkness dissipated. The teenagers found themselves standing in a field of withered corn stalks, surrounded by the twisted and mangled bodies of their friends and neighbors.

As they tried to flee, they realized that the town had been sacrificed to a dark force that demanded an annual harvest of human souls. And now, they too were a part of the Dark Harvest Festival, forever trapped in a never-ending cycle of death and sacrifice.

Chapter 19

The House That Time Forgot

Caroline had always been fascinated by the abandoned house at the edge of town. It was a grand old mansion that had once belonged to a wealthy family, but now it was nothing more than a decaying relic of a forgotten era.

One day, Caroline decided to explore the house. She pushed open the front door and stepped inside, her footsteps echoing through the empty rooms. The air was thick with the musty scent of neglect, and cobwebs hung from the ceilings like drapes.

As she wandered through the house, Caroline noticed something strange. Despite the obvious signs of decay and neglect, everything in the house appeared to be frozen in time. The furniture was still arranged as though it was waiting for guests to arrive, and the portraits on the walls stared out with blank expressions.

As she explored further, Caroline found herself drawn to a locked room on the third floor. She could hear faint whispers and footsteps coming from within, and she was determined to uncover the secrets hidden inside.

She searched the house for a key, but there was none to be found. Finally, in frustration, she kicked the door down.

Inside the room, Caroline found herself transported to another era. The room was lavishly decorated, with fine silk curtains and ornate furniture. A woman in a flowing gown stood before her, her eyes filled with terror.

"Who are you?" Caroline asked, but the woman didn't answer. Instead, she disappeared through a hidden door.

Caroline followed the woman through the door and found herself in a labyrinthine maze of corridors and rooms. She could hear the woman's footsteps echoing through the halls, and she followed the sound until she found herself in a room filled with mirrors.

As Caroline gazed into the mirrors, she saw images of herself from different times and places. She realized that the house had trapped her in a time loop, and that she was doomed to wander its halls forever.

The woman appeared before her once more, her face twisted into a rictus of fear. "You can never leave," she whispered, before disappearing once more.

Caroline screamed in terror as the house's grip tightened around her, trapping her in a never-ending cycle of time and horror.

Chapter 20

The Night the Dead Came to Life

It was just another night at the cemetery for Tom, the caretaker. He was used to the quiet and solitude, spending his nights among the graves and mausoleums. But tonight, something was different. The air was thick with an unnatural stillness, and Tom felt like he was being watched.

As he went about his duties, Tom heard strange noises coming from the ground. At first, he thought it was just the wind, but then he heard a low moaning that seemed to be coming from the graves themselves.

Suddenly, the ground began to shake and the soil around the graves began to move. Tom watched in horror as the dead bodies clawed their way out of the earth, their flesh rotting and their eyes glowing with a sickly green light.

Tom tried to run, but he was surrounded on all sides by the walking dead. They swarmed over him, their cold, clammy hands grasping at his flesh as he struggled to break free.

Just when it seemed like all was lost, a group of survivors arrived on the scene, armed with makeshift weapons and determined to fight back against the undead hordes. Tom joined forces with them, fighting side by side as they battled the zombie apocalypse that had descended upon their town.

Together, they fought their way through the cemetery, battling zombies and uncovering the dark secret behind the undead outbreak. In the end, they were able to destroy the source of the infection and send the zombies back to their graves.

But for Tom, the memory of that night would haunt him forever. He knew that the dead could come back to life, and he would never feel safe among the graves again.

Chapter 21

The Vengeful Ghost of Emily James

When the James family moved into their new house, they didn't know what they were getting into. They had heard rumors of a ghost that haunted the place, but they had dismissed them as idle gossip. That was until they met Emily James.

Emily had died in the house years before, and her spirit had never left. She had been wronged in life, and she wasn't going to let anyone forget it.

At first, the family experienced only minor disturbances: doors opening and closing on their own, strange noises in the night, and cold spots that seemed to move around the house. But as time passed, Emily's ghost grew more and more angry. Objects flew off shelves, furniture moved on its own, and the family began to feel a sense of unease whenever they were alone in the house.

One night, as the family was gathered in the living room watching TV, they heard a loud crash upstairs. They rushed to investigate and found that Emily's old bedroom had been completely destroyed. The walls were covered in scratches and blood, and the furniture was smashed to pieces.

As they stood there in shock, they felt a cold breeze blow past them. They turned to see Emily's ghost standing before them, her eyes blazing with anger. She had been wronged in life, and now she was going to get her revenge.

The family tried to flee the house, but Emily's ghost wouldn't let them leave. She appeared before them at every turn, haunting their dreams and tormenting them with visions of their own deaths.

In the end, the family had to confront their own past and the wrongs they had committed against Emily. They had to make amends before she would finally let them go.

But even now, years later, the family can still feel Emily's ghost watching over them, a constant reminder of the consequences of their actions. They learned the

hard way that some ghosts never forgive, and never
forget.

Chapter 22

The Island of the Damned

It was supposed to be a relaxing vacation on a tropical
island paradise. But as soon as the group of tourists
stepped off the boat onto the shore, they knew
something was wrong.

The air was thick with a putrid odor, and the trees were
twisted and gnarled, as if they were reaching out to
grab them. The island was completely deserted, and
there was no sign of the hotel they had booked their
stay in.

As they made their way through the jungle, they heard
strange whispers and moans coming from the trees.
They were being watched, and they knew it.

When they finally stumbled upon the hotel, they realized too late that they had made a grave mistake. The building was dilapidated and covered in vines, and the staff was nowhere to be found.

As night fell, the group heard unearthly screams and cries coming from deep within the jungle. They huddled together, praying for dawn to come.

But when the sun rose, they found themselves trapped on the island, unable to leave. The boat that had brought them there was gone, and the water surrounding the island was filled with deadly creatures.

As they explored the island, they found evidence of a horrific past. The hotel had once been a mental asylum, where unspeakable acts of torture and experimentation had taken place.

The spirits of the tortured patients still lingered on the island, seeking revenge on anyone who dared to set foot on their cursed land. The group knew that they had to find a way off the island before they became the next victims of the damned.

But as they struggled to survive, they realized that they may never escape the island alive. The spirits were relentless, and their torment would never end. The island of the damned had claimed yet another group of unsuspecting victims.

Chapter 23

The Midnight Caller

It was well past midnight when the phone rang in Rachel's apartment. She picked it up groggily, expecting to hear the voice of a drunk dialer or a wrong number. Instead, she was met with a chilling silence on the other end.

"Hello?" she said, her voice quivering.

There was no response, but Rachel could hear something breathing on the other end of the line. It was ragged and heavy, like the breath of a dying animal.

"Who is this?" she asked, her heart pounding in her chest.

Still, there was no answer, but the breathing grew louder, filling the room with a suffocating presence.

Rachel hung up the phone and tried to calm herself down, telling herself that it was just a prank call or a wrong number. But then the phone rang again, and again, and again, each time with the same heavy breathing on the other end.

As the night wore on, the calls became more frequent and the breathing more sinister. Rachel tried to ignore them, but they seemed to follow her everywhere she went, even into her dreams.

When she woke up the next morning, Rachel was exhausted and terrified. She knew she had to do something to stop the calls, but she didn't know where to turn. She went to the police, but they couldn't trace the calls and told her there was nothing they could do.

Desperate for a solution, Rachel turned to a local psychic who specialized in dealing with the supernatural. The psychic listened carefully to Rachel's story and then revealed a terrifying truth: the caller was not of this world, but a vengeful spirit who had been wronged in life and was seeking revenge.

Rachel was horrified, but the psychic offered to help her banish the spirit and end the calls once and for all. Together, they performed a ritual that involved burning sage and reciting ancient incantations.

As they finished the ritual, the room filled with a blinding light and the air grew heavy with the presence of the spirit. But then, just as suddenly as it had appeared, the spirit was gone, and the calls stopped.

Rachel never heard from the midnight caller again, but she knew that the memory of that night would haunt her forever. She had come face to face with a force beyond her understanding, and she knew that there were darker, more malevolent entities lurking in the shadows, waiting to claim their next victim.

Chapter 24

The Legend of the Bloody Bride

The small town of Ravenwood had always been shrouded in mystery and superstition. But when a group of teenagers stumbled upon the legend of the Bloody Bride, they knew they had to investigate.

The story went that many years ago, a young woman named Isabella had been forced into an arranged marriage with a wealthy landowner. On her wedding day, Isabella was found dead in her bridal suite, her body covered in blood and her throat slit from ear to ear.

Since then, it was said that on the anniversary of her death, the ghost of the Bloody Bride would appear in the abandoned mansion where she had lived with her husband. Her wailing cries could be heard echoing through the halls, and those who saw her would be cursed to die a violent death.

Undeterred by the warnings, the teenagers made their way to the abandoned mansion on the night of the anniversary. As they entered the dilapidated building, they heard the sound of a woman weeping, and the air grew thick with the scent of roses.

Suddenly, the room was filled with a blinding light, and a figure appeared before them. It was Isabella, her white wedding dress stained with blood and her eyes filled with fury.

The teenagers tried to run, but the doors and windows had all been sealed shut. They were trapped with the vengeful spirit, who floated towards them with a dagger in hand.

One by one, the teenagers were picked off by the Bloody Bride, their screams echoing through the mansion. And as the sun rose on the anniversary of Isabella's death, the mansion was silent once more.

But the legend of the Bloody Bride lived on, a warning to those who dared to enter Ravenwood and disturb the dead.

Chapter 25

The Cursed Forest of Lost Souls

When Rachel and her friends stumbled upon the old map showing the location of the Cursed Forest of Lost Souls, they couldn't resist the lure of adventure. They packed their bags and set out into the wilderness, determined to find the ancient burial site rumored to contain untold riches.

As they entered the forest, they felt a sense of unease wash over them. The trees seemed to loom over them, their twisted branches reaching out like skeletal fingers. Strange noises echoed through the woods, and they caught glimpses of movement out of the corners of their eyes.

The group pressed on, their determination to find the treasure outweighing their fear. But as the days wore on, they began to feel as though they were being watched. They heard whispers on the wind, and saw shadowy figures darting through the trees.

One night, as they set up camp, they heard a bloodcurdling scream coming from the woods. They rushed to investigate, but found nothing except for a strange symbol carved into a nearby tree.

As they continued deeper into the forest, they began to lose their sense of direction. They stumbled upon an ancient stone altar, covered in strange runes and symbols. The air grew thick with an otherworldly presence, and they knew they had stumbled upon something far more dangerous than they had ever imagined.

Suddenly, a figure stepped out from behind the altar, its eyes glowing with an otherworldly light. It spoke to them in a language they could not understand, and they knew they were in the presence of an ancient and malevolent force.

The group tried to run, but they found themselves lost in the maze-like forest. They heard screams and whispers coming from all around them, and knew that they would never escape the curse of the forest of lost souls. They had dared to seek what was forbidden, and now they would pay the ultimate price.

Chapter 26

The Scream Queen's Revenge

Maggie had always dreamed of being a horror movie star, and she had finally achieved her goal by playing the lead role in "Scream Queen", a low-budget slasher flick. But her moment of triumph was short-lived, as the film's director, Todd, had taken all the credit for her success.

Furious at being overlooked, Maggie decided to take matters into her own hands. She snuck into the studio after hours and began to wreak havoc on the set, destroying props and slashing through the fake blood with a real knife.

But as she made her way through the set, she heard strange whispers and creaking sounds coming from the shadows. She dismissed them as her imagination and continued her rampage until she heard a scream coming from Todd's office.

Maggie rushed in to find Todd lying on the ground, his throat cut open. She saw a figure in the corner of the room, dressed in a torn and bloody costume, holding a real machete. It was the killer from the movie, but he was supposed to be just a prop.

The figure turned to Maggie and spoke in a low, guttural voice, "You should have given me credit, Maggie. Now, I'm going to give you the role of a lifetime."

The killer lunged at Maggie, who barely managed to dodge the machete. She ran out of the office and into the darkened soundstage, where she was trapped with the crazed killer. They played a game of cat and mouse, with Maggie using her wits to outsmart the killer at every turn.

As dawn broke, the police arrived and subdued the killer, who turned out to be one of Todd's disgruntled former employees. Maggie was hailed as a hero and given the credit she deserved for her performance in the film.

But as she walked away from the studio, she couldn't shake the feeling that something was watching her from the shadows. She turned to see the killer's mask lying on the ground, staring back at her with empty eye holes. Maggie knew that the Scream Queen's revenge was far from over.

Chapter 27

The Witch of Whispering Woods

When a group of friends decided to go camping in the Whispering Woods, they had no idea they would encounter a witch who had been banished from the nearby town centuries ago.

As they sat around the campfire, telling ghost stories and roasting marshmallows, they heard a faint whispering in the trees. At first, they thought it was just the wind, but as the whispers grew louder, they realized it was something far more sinister.

Suddenly, a figure emerged from the woods, her long hair trailing behind her as she approached the group. She introduced herself as the Witch of Whispering Woods and demanded to know what they were doing on her land.

The group tried to explain that they were just camping and meant no harm, but the witch was not convinced. She claimed that the woods were her domain and that any intruders would be punished severely.

As the night wore on, strange things began to happen. Their tent collapsed inexplicably, and their supplies went missing. They heard screams and whispers in the darkness, and the witch's cackling laughter echoed through the trees.

It soon became clear that the witch was not going to let them leave the woods alive. She revealed that she had been banished from the nearby town for practicing dark magic and that she had been seeking revenge ever since.

The group tried to flee, but the witch's magic was too powerful. They found themselves lost in the woods, with no way out and the witch's dark presence closing in on them.

In a last-ditch effort to escape, the group decided to confront the witch head-on. They gathered what supplies they had left and set a trap for her.

As the witch approached, they sprang the trap, using a combination of fire and holy water to drive her back. The witch screamed in rage and agony as she vanished into the darkness, never to be seen again.

The group emerged from the woods shaken but alive, knowing that they had narrowly escaped the clutches of the Witch of Whispering Woods. But they also knew that the woods would never be the same again, and that the witch's dark magic would continue to haunt the forest for years to come.

Chapter 28

The Killer in the Cornfield

Every year, the small town of Millfield held a corn maze festival to celebrate the harvest season. Families from all over the area would come to get lost in the maze and enjoy the local food and festivities.

But this year, something was different. As the sun began to set and the maze grew darker, screams could be heard coming from deep within the cornfield. Parents frantically searched for their children as the sound of a chainsaw echoed through the maze.

As the chaos ensued, a group of teenagers decided to investigate. Armed with nothing but their wits and a few flashlights, they plunged deeper into the maze, determined to find the source of the commotion.

As they neared the center of the maze, they saw him. A man with a chainsaw, dressed in a burlap sack and overalls, was chasing down festival-goers and brutally attacking them.

The teenagers quickly realized that this was not a part of the festival's entertainment, but a real-life horror show. They had stumbled upon a deranged killer who had hidden himself in the maze.

One by one, the teenagers fell victim to the killer's attacks. The cornstalks rustled as he chased after them with his chainsaw, relentlessly hunting them down until there was only one left.

The final teenager managed to outsmart the killer, leading him into a trap and subduing him with a well-placed blow to the head. As the police arrived on the scene, they uncovered a chilling discovery. The killer had been living in the cornfield for months, using the maze to lure victims to their deaths.

The town was forever changed by the events of that night, and the corn maze festival was never held again. But the memory of the killer in the cornfield would haunt the town's residents for years to come.

Chapter 29

The Specter of Stonehurst Cemetery

For as long as anyone in the small town of Millfield could remember, the old Stonehurst Cemetery had been a place of deep unease. Legends told of ghosts and spirits that roamed the grounds, and many locals avoided the place altogether after dark.

But when a rash of disappearances began to plague the town, all eyes turned to Stonehurst Cemetery as the possible source of the terror.

One night, a group of teenagers decided to investigate the rumors for themselves. They entered the cemetery just as the sun began to set, the sky turning a deep shade of red as they made their way through the overgrown graves.

As they reached the center of the cemetery, they saw something that made their blood run cold. A dark figure stood before them, its eyes glowing like hot coals in the fading light.

Before they could flee, the figure raised its hands and let out a piercing scream. The ground beneath the teenagers began to shake and the graves opened up, releasing a horde of undead spirits.

The teenagers ran for their lives, pursued by the spectral horde through the twisting paths of the cemetery. They stumbled and fell, but managed to keep ahead of the relentless pursuit.

Finally, they reached the edge of the cemetery, only to find their way blocked by the dark figure they had seen earlier. It reached out and grabbed one of the teenagers, its icy grip paralyzing him with fear.

But then, something strange happened. The figure's form began to dissolve, revealing a young girl who had died many years before in a tragic accident. She spoke to the teenagers in a mournful voice, telling them that her spirit had been trapped in the cemetery by a curse, and that she needed their help to break it.

Together, the teenagers performed a ritual that lifted the curse and set the spirits of Stonehurst Cemetery free. The girl's spirit finally found peace, and the town of Millfield was never plagued by disappearances again. But the memory of that night lingered on, a reminder of the horrors that could lie just beneath the surface of even the most peaceful-looking places.

Chapter 30

The House of Horrors

As soon as the group stepped inside the house, they knew something was wrong. The air was thick with the smell of decay and the walls were adorned with disturbing artwork and strange symbols.

As they made their way through the maze-like hallways, they heard the sound of a woman's screams coming from somewhere deep within the house. They followed the noise until they reached a room filled with torture devices and blood-stained walls.

In the center of the room stood a woman, her body contorted and twisted in pain as she was stretched on a rack. A man in a hooded cloak stood beside her, his eyes glinting with malevolence.

Without warning, the man turned to face the group, and they could see that his face was covered in gruesome scars and burns. He brandished a large knife and began to advance on them, his laughter echoing through the house.

The group scattered, trying to find a way out of the maze-like house, but they found themselves trapped in a labyrinth of twisting corridors and locked doors.

As they ran, they stumbled upon more rooms filled with horrors beyond their imagination. They saw bodies suspended from the ceiling, twisted and contorted into grotesque shapes. They saw walls lined with jars filled with strange and unsettling contents.

Their only hope was to find a way out before the madman caught up with them. As they ran, they finally came upon a door that led outside.

As they burst through the door, they found themselves in a clearing surrounded by trees. But as they looked back at the house, they saw that it was no ordinary house. It was a living, breathing entity, pulsating with malevolent energy.

The group knew that they had stumbled upon something far beyond their understanding, something that should never have been disturbed. And they knew that the House of Horrors would continue to haunt them for the rest of their lives.

Chapter 31

The Dollhouse Murders

Sophie had always been fascinated by dollhouses. She loved the intricacy of the tiny furniture and the attention to detail in every miniature room. So when she inherited a dollhouse from her great-aunt, she was overjoyed.

But as Sophie began to play with the dollhouse, strange things started to happen. The dolls seemed to move on their own, their expressions changing from benign to malevolent when no one was looking. Sophie tried to dismiss it as her imagination, but she couldn't shake the feeling that something was watching her.

One night, Sophie was awakened by a sound coming from the dollhouse. She went to investigate, but as she opened the door, she was attacked by a swarm of tiny dolls. They clawed at her flesh with tiny razor-sharp teeth, their eyes glowing with a malevolent light.

Sophie managed to escape the dollhouse, but the terror didn't end there. In the days that followed, Sophie began to hear rumors of a series of grisly murders, each victim found torn apart by tiny claws and teeth.

As Sophie investigated further, she realized that the dollhouse was connected to the murders. The tiny furniture and decor in the dollhouse matched the rooms where the victims were found, and the dolls themselves resembled the killers.

Sophie knew she had to destroy the dollhouse before it claimed any more victims, but she couldn't do it alone. With the help of a group of friends, Sophie returned to the dollhouse and waged a desperate battle against the tiny, malevolent dolls.

In the end, they were victorious, but at a terrible cost. Sophie and her friends had been scarred by the experience, haunted by the knowledge that something so innocent could turn so deadly. The dollhouse lay shattered and broken, but the memory of the Dollhouse Murders would stay with them forever.

Chapter 32

The Curse of the Black Cat

It was a moonless night when Emily and her boyfriend, Jake, stumbled upon an old abandoned mansion deep in the woods. They were both thrill-seekers, always on the lookout for a new adventure, and the dilapidated mansion seemed like the perfect place to explore.

As they entered the mansion, they were greeted by a strange sight - a black cat with glowing eyes staring at them from the top of the stairs. Despite feeling uneasy, they brushed off their fear and continued exploring the mansion.

As they ventured further into the mansion, strange things began to happen. Doors would open and close on their own, and they heard strange whispers coming from the shadows. The black cat seemed to be following them everywhere they went, its glowing eyes watching their every move.

Suddenly, Jake was overcome with a sense of dread. He felt like something was crawling under his skin, and he couldn't shake the feeling that they were being watched by something far more sinister than just a black cat.

As they turned a corner, they found themselves face to face with a hooded figure, its eyes glowing in the darkness. The figure beckoned them closer, and as they approached, they saw that it was holding a black cat in its arms.

The figure spoke in a voice that seemed to come from the depths of hell, warning them of the curse that had befallen the mansion. The black cat was a manifestation of the curse, and it would never let them leave the mansion alive.

Emily and Jake tried to flee, but the black cat seemed to be everywhere, blocking their path and leading them deeper into the mansion. They heard the sound of chanting and saw figures in black robes performing some kind of ritual.

As the night wore on, Emily and Jake realized that they were trapped in the mansion, and that the only way to break the curse was to confront the source of the evil that had taken hold. They had to find a way to defeat the black cat and the hooded figure that controlled it, or risk being trapped forever in the cursed mansion.

Chapter 33

The Ghostly Guardian of Glenwood Manor

When Emily inherited Glenwood Manor from her grandfather, she had no idea of the horrors that lay within its walls. As she moved in and began to explore the sprawling estate, she felt a sense of unease that she couldn't shake off.

One night, as she was walking through the garden, she heard a faint whisper in her ear. She turned around, but there was no one there. She dismissed it as her imagination and continued on her way, but as she walked deeper into the garden, the whispers grew louder and more insistent.

Suddenly, she saw a figure materialize before her, its face twisted in an expression of anger and malice. It was the ghostly guardian of Glenwood Manor, the spirit of her grandfather's loyal servant who had been murdered in the manor years before.

The ghostly guardian warned Emily to leave the manor, telling her that it was cursed and that she would be in danger if she stayed. Emily refused to believe him, thinking that he was just a figment of her imagination. But as the days passed, she began to experience more and more strange occurrences, from doors slamming shut on their own to shadows moving across the walls.

One night, Emily woke up to find the ghostly guardian standing at the foot of her bed. He told her that he had been watching over her, trying to protect her from the malevolent spirits that haunted the manor. He begged her to leave before it was too late, but Emily was too stubborn to listen.

As the days turned into weeks, Emily began to feel as though she was being watched at all times. She could hear whispers and footsteps echoing through the empty halls, and every time she turned a corner, she felt as though something was waiting for her.

Finally, Emily could take it no longer. She packed her bags and fled from Glenwood Manor, leaving behind the ghostly guardian and the malevolent spirits that haunted its halls. But as she looked back at the manor from a distance, she knew that she had not escaped its curse completely. The ghostly guardian still watched over the manor, waiting for the next unsuspecting victim to fall under its deadly spell.

Chapter 34

The Bloodstained Bride

On the outskirts of town, there stood an old mansion that had been abandoned for years. The locals whispered that the mansion was cursed, that anyone who entered it would never return. But when Lucy's sister, Lily, went missing after going to the mansion for a late-night party, Lucy knew she had to investigate.

As she entered the mansion's grand ballroom, she saw a figure in a tattered wedding dress standing at the far end of the room. The figure's face was obscured by a veil, and her hands were stained with blood.

Lucy approached the bride cautiously, her heart racing with fear. The bride beckoned her closer, and as Lucy got within arm's reach, the bride grabbed her wrist with surprising strength.

Suddenly, Lucy was surrounded by the ghosts of brides past, their ghostly moans filling the room. They told her their stories, of how they had been lured to the mansion by promises of love and happiness, only to be murdered by their deranged fiancé.

Lucy felt a chill run down her spine as she realized that the bloodstained bride was none other than Lily's killer. She struggled to break free from the bride's grasp, but the ghostly brides held her tight.

Just when it seemed like all was lost, Lucy remembered the old legend of the mansion. She called out to the spirit of the mansion itself, challenging it to release her from its grasp.

With a deafening roar, the mansion's walls began to shake and the ghostly brides were forced to release Lucy. She made a mad dash for the exit, narrowly escaping the cursed mansion and the bloodstained bride.

As she stumbled into the night air, Lucy knew that she had uncovered the truth about her sister's disappearance. But she also knew that the memory of the bloodstained bride and the cursed mansion would haunt her for the rest of her days.

Chapter 35

The Demon's Den

Rachel and her friends had been hiking for hours through the dense forest, searching for the hidden cave that was rumored to lead to the Demon's Den. They had heard stories of the dark forces that lurked within the cave, but they were determined to explore it anyway.

As they approached the entrance, they felt a chill run down their spines. The air was thick with the stench of decay, and the walls were covered in strange symbols and markings.

They pushed deeper into the cave, their flashlights illuminating the way. The sound of dripping water echoed through the narrow passages, and they could hear strange whispers and whispers coming from deep within the darkness.

Suddenly, they saw a figure standing in the shadows ahead. It was tall and gaunt, with eyes that glowed like hot coals. They tried to run, but it was too late - the figure had already caught them in its grasp.

The demon dragged them deeper into the cave, past twisting tunnels and gaping chasms. They saw unspeakable horrors along the way - piles of bones, dark pools of blood, and strange, otherworldly creatures that slithered and crawled in the darkness.

As they reached the heart of the demon's den, Rachel and her friends were thrown into a pit of fire and brimstone. They screamed in agony as the flames consumed them, their bodies twisting and contorting as the demon's power flowed through them.

When they emerged from the pit, they were no longer themselves. They were vessels for the demon's evil, spreading chaos and destruction wherever they went.

Rachel knew then that they had made a terrible mistake. They had entered the Demon's Den seeking knowledge and power, but all they had found was damnation. They were trapped in a nightmare world of darkness and terror, and there was no escape.

Chapter 36

The Children of the Cornstalks

It was harvest season in the small farming town of Millfield, and the fields were ripe with golden cornstalks. But as the sun set on the first day of the harvest, strange things began to happen. The cornstalks seemed to come alive, bending and twisting in unnatural ways, and eerie whispers could be heard on the wind.

The townspeople were uneasy, but they brushed it off as their imaginations getting the best of them. But when the children of the town started disappearing, they knew something was seriously wrong.

One night, a group of concerned parents set out to search for their missing children. As they made their way through the cornfields, they heard the sound of laughter and singing coming from a nearby clearing.

What they found there chilled them to the bone. A group of children, their faces painted in grotesque designs, were dancing and chanting around a large bonfire. But as the parents approached, the children turned to face them, their eyes glowing with an otherworldly light.

The children revealed that they had made a pact with the cornstalks, offering sacrifices in exchange for a bountiful harvest. The cornstalks had granted them powers beyond their wildest dreams, and now the children were determined to protect their newfound source of power at any cost.

The parents tried to reason with the children, but it was no use. The children had been corrupted by the darkness that lurked within the cornfields, and they would stop at nothing to defend their new way of life.

As the parents retreated, they could hear the children's eerie laughter echoing through the cornfields, and they knew that Millfield would never be the same again. The children of the cornstalks had claimed the town as their own, and anyone who dared to cross them would suffer a terrible fate.

Chapter 37

The Midnight Curse of Moonlight Manor

It was a warm summer night when Maria and her friends decided to sneak into Moonlight Manor, a sprawling estate on the outskirts of town that had been abandoned for years. They had heard rumors of a powerful curse that had befallen the estate and its inhabitants, and they were determined to uncover the truth.

As they approached the manor, the moon shone brightly overhead, casting an eerie glow over the overgrown gardens and crumbling walls. The group snuck through the broken fence and made their way towards the front door, their hearts pounding with excitement and fear.

The door creaked open as they pushed it aside, revealing a grand foyer filled with cobwebs and dust. Maria led the way as they explored the sprawling mansion, their flashlights illuminating the faded paintings and ornate furniture.

As they climbed the stairs, they heard strange whispers and creaks coming from the empty rooms. Maria felt a cold breeze brush against her neck, and she knew they were not alone in the mansion.

Suddenly, the floorboards beneath them began to tremble, and the walls started to crack. Maria and her friends realized too late that they had disturbed the ancient curse that had been lying dormant within the manor for years.

The group ran for their lives as the mansion began to collapse around them, the curse unleashing its full fury upon them. They were pursued by spectral apparitions and monstrous creatures, each one more terrifying than the last.

As they reached the front door, they thought they had made it to safety. But the curse had other plans. The door slammed shut behind them, trapping them within the manor's cursed walls forever.

Maria and her friends screamed in terror as they realized the true horror of their situation. They had become trapped in Moonlight Manor, cursed to wander its halls and suffer the same fate as its previous inhabitants. The curse of the manor had claimed them, and they would never be free again.

Chapter 38

The Possession of Mary Brown

Mary Brown was always a devout and pious woman. She went to church every Sunday, prayed before every meal, and never missed an opportunity to do a good deed. But one day, something changed.

As Mary was walking home from the grocery store, she felt a strange sensation come over her. It was as if something had taken hold of her body and was guiding her movements. She felt herself being led to an old abandoned church on the outskirts of town.

Inside the church, Mary was confronted by a sinister presence. It spoke to her in a voice that was not her own, promising her power and riches beyond her wildest dreams. Mary tried to resist, but the presence was too strong.

Over the next few days, Mary's behavior grew increasingly erratic. She started speaking in tongues, convulsing violently, and exhibiting other signs of possession. Her husband called in a priest to perform an exorcism, but the demon inside Mary proved to be too powerful.

As the days turned into weeks, Mary's possession became more and more pronounced. She began to exhibit strange powers, such as telekinesis and mind control. People around her started to disappear under mysterious circumstances, and rumors began to spread that Mary was responsible.

Finally, a group of concerned citizens banded together to take matters into their own hands. They stormed the church where Mary was being held, determined to put an end to the possession once and for all.

But when they arrived, they found something that they never could have expected. Mary was not possessed by a demon, but by a powerful witch who had been using her body as a vessel to carry out her evil deeds.

In a final showdown, the group battled the witch and her minions, using all their strength and wits to overcome their dark powers. When the smoke cleared, Mary lay unconscious on the floor, free from the possession that had tormented her for so long.

But the victory came at a steep price. Many had lost their lives in the battle, and the town was left in shambles. As the survivors began to pick up the pieces and rebuild, they knew that they would never forget the terror that had befallen them at the hands of the witch who had possessed Mary Brown.

Chapter 39

The Whispering Woman of the Windmill

It had been a long day of hiking through the woods, and Jane and her husband Tom were relieved to come across the old windmill at the edge of the clearing. They decided to spend the night there, enjoying the shelter it provided from the cold and damp night air.

As they settled in for the night, they began to hear strange whispers coming from within the windmill. The whispers were soft and barely audible, but they seemed to be coming from a woman's voice.

Jane and Tom tried to ignore the whispers and go to sleep, but the sound continued to grow louder and more insistent. It was as if the woman was trying to tell them something, but her words were jumbled and incoherent.

Eventually, Jane and Tom got up to investigate the source of the whispers. As they entered the upper level of the windmill, they saw a figure standing in the corner, shrouded in shadows.

The figure was that of a woman, but her features were obscured by the darkness. She continued to whisper incoherently, her voice rising and falling like the wind outside.

Suddenly, the figure turned towards them and let out a blood-curdling scream. Her face was twisted into a grotesque mask of rage and hatred, and her eyes seemed to glow with an otherworldly light.

Jane and Tom tried to run, but the woman's grip was too strong. She pulled them back towards her, whispering unintelligibly in their ears as they struggled in terror.

Finally, they managed to break free and flee from the windmill, never looking back. But the memory of the whispering woman would haunt them for the rest of their lives, a reminder of the evil that lurked in the darkness of the world.

Chapter 40

The Haunted Hotel on the Hill

The old hotel on the hill had been abandoned for years, ever since the mysterious disappearance of its owner and all of its guests. But for Marie and her friends, the rumors of the hotel's haunting only added to its allure.

They arrived at the hotel on a cold and foggy night, their breath visible in the chill air. The once-grand building was now dilapidated and covered in cobwebs, and the windows were shattered and boarded up.

As they made their way through the lobby, they heard whispers and footsteps coming from the upper floors. But they were undeterred, eager to explore the hotel's dark secrets.

They climbed the stairs, their flashlights flickering as they moved deeper into the hotel's depths. The air grew colder and the darkness more oppressive, until they reached a door at the end of the hallway.

As they pushed it open, they found themselves in a grand ballroom, its chandeliers dimly glowing in the darkness. But the room was not empty - there were ghosts everywhere, twirling and spinning in a macabre dance.

Marie and her friends watched in horror as the ghosts turned towards them, their faces twisted in agony and despair. They reached out, their spectral hands passing through Marie's body like ice.

Suddenly, the ghosts disappeared, replaced by a single figure standing in the center of the room. It was the hotel's former owner, his eyes glowing with an otherworldly light.

He beckoned to them, his voice a hollow whisper. "Join us," he said. "Become a part of this place, forever trapped in its haunted halls."

Marie and her friends tried to run, but the door slammed shut behind them, trapping them in the ballroom with the ghostly figure. They knew they had made a grave mistake in coming to the haunted hotel on the hill, and that they may never leave alive.

Chapter 41

The Soul Eater's Sanctuary

Nina had always been fascinated by the stories of the Soul Eater's Sanctuary. It was said to be a place where the most powerful demons gathered to feast on the souls of the living. Nina never believed in such tales, but when her brother went missing in the area, she decided to investigate.

As she made her way through the dense forest, she noticed that the trees seemed to twist and writhe as if alive. The air grew thick with the stench of rotting flesh, and the ground became slick with blood. She heard the distant sounds of chanting and the occasional scream.

Finally, she stumbled upon the entrance to the Sanctuary, a massive stone archway with demonic symbols etched into its surface. Beyond it, she could see a vast chamber filled with flickering torches and strange, twisted statues.

Nina cautiously entered the chamber, her footsteps echoing through the cavernous space. Suddenly, she heard a voice whisper her name. She turned to see a figure draped in black robes, its face obscured by shadows.

The figure introduced itself as the Soul Eater, and offered Nina a deal. In exchange for her soul, it would grant her the power to find her brother and return him to the world of the living.

Nina hesitated, but the Soul Eater's words were too tempting to ignore. She agreed to the deal and felt a surge of power coursing through her veins. She followed the Soul Eater through a labyrinth of tunnels and chambers, her senses overwhelmed by the sights and sounds around her.

Finally, they reached a chamber where her brother lay unconscious on an altar, surrounded by a circle of demons. The Soul Eater instructed Nina to take her brother's place on the altar, but she refused.

Enraged, the Soul Eater unleashed a wave of dark energy that sent Nina flying across the room. As she lay battered and bruised, she realized the true nature of the Soul Eater's Sanctuary. It was not a place of power, but a trap for the unwary, a place where the most desperate could be lured to their doom.

With a final burst of strength, Nina used her newfound powers to banish the Soul Eater and the demons back to their realm. She gathered her brother in her arms and fled the Sanctuary, vowing to never again dabble in the dark arts.

Chapter 42

The Shadowy Stranger on the Subway

It was a typical evening commute for Emily as she boarded the subway train. The car was nearly empty, with only a few tired-looking passengers scattered throughout. Emily took a seat near the center of the car and began to lose herself in a book, grateful for the chance to unwind after a long day at work.

As the train pulled into the next station, a tall figure stepped onto the car. Emily couldn't make out his face, as he was shrouded in a long, black cloak that seemed to swallow the light around him. She couldn't help but feel uneasy at his presence, but tried to dismiss her fears as irrational.

The stranger took a seat across from her, and Emily couldn't shake the feeling that he was watching her. She tried to ignore him and return to her book, but found her eyes wandering back to him again and again.

Suddenly, the lights flickered and went out, plunging the car into darkness. Emily heard the other passengers gasping in surprise and fear, but before she could react, she felt a cold hand on her shoulder.

She turned to see the stranger leaning towards her, his face still obscured by the hood of his cloak. He whispered something in a language she didn't recognize, and she felt a chill run down her spine.

As the lights flickered back on, Emily saw that the stranger had vanished, leaving only a small, black feather in his place. She tried to shake off the fear and confusion that gripped her, but couldn't shake the feeling that something was deeply wrong.

Over the next few days, Emily began to experience strange and terrifying nightmares. In each one, she saw the shadowy figure from the subway, lurking in the shadows and whispering in that same strange language. She couldn't escape the feeling that he was trying to communicate something to her, something dark and dangerous.

Finally, unable to take it any longer, Emily sought out the help of a psychic medium. Together, they performed a ritual to contact the spirit realm, and Emily saw the shadowy figure once again, looming over her in a swirl of dark energy.

It was then that she realized the truth: the stranger on the subway was not a man at all, but a demon, sent to torment her and drag her down into the darkness. With the help of the psychic medium, Emily was able to banish the demon back to the depths from whence it came, but she knew she would never forget the terror of that encounter on the subway.

Chapter 43

The Chanting Cult of Candlewood Creek

The town of Candlewood Creek was known for its picturesque countryside and idyllic way of life. But beneath the surface, there was a dark and sinister secret. A cult had taken root in the town, and they were performing unspeakable rituals in the dead of night.

When Emma arrived in town to investigate reports of strange occurrences, she had no idea what she was getting into. She soon discovered that the cult was led by a charismatic and enigmatic figure known only as The Prophet.

Emma's investigation led her to a remote clearing in the woods, where she witnessed the cult's dark rituals first-hand. They chanted in a language she didn't understand, their eyes closed in ecstasy as they danced around a raging fire.

As she watched in horror, Emma realized that the cult was preparing to sacrifice a young woman to their dark gods. Emma knew she had to act fast if she was going to save the girl's life.

She crept closer to the cultists, careful not to alert them to her presence. When she was close enough, she launched herself at The Prophet, hoping to disrupt the ritual and save the young woman.

But as she grappled with The Prophet, Emma realized that he was no ordinary man. He possessed incredible strength and agility, and his eyes seemed to glow with a malevolent energy.

The cultists closed in around her, their chants growing louder and more frenzied. Emma knew she was in grave danger and that she needed to find a way to escape before it was too late.

With all her might, Emma broke free from The Prophet's grasp and ran towards the woods. The cultists chased after her, their chants echoing through the trees.

Emma stumbled through the underbrush, her heart pounding in her chest. She could hear the cultists getting closer and closer, and she knew that she had to find a way to stop them once and for all.

With a burst of energy, Emma emerged from the woods and ran towards the nearest town. She knew that she had to warn the authorities about the cult before it was too late.

As she stumbled into the local police station, Emma realized that she had just narrowly escaped with her life. But she also knew that the Chanting Cult of Candlewood Creek was still out there, waiting for its next victim.

Chapter 44

The Butcher of Briarwood Farm

For years, the people of Briarwood had whispered about the strange happenings at the old farm on the outskirts of town. Some said that the land was cursed, that it had been built on an ancient burial ground. Others spoke of a strange man who lived on the farm, who never spoke to anyone and only came into town once a month to buy supplies.

But it wasn't until the bodies started showing up that the town truly realized the horror that lay hidden at Briarwood Farm.

The first body was discovered by a group of teenagers who had been hiking in the woods near the farm. It was the body of a young woman, her throat slashed and her body mutilated beyond recognition. The town was shaken by the gruesome discovery, but it was only the beginning.

Over the next few months, more bodies were found. Each one was a young woman, each one killed in the same brutal and horrific manner. The town was gripped by fear, and rumors of a serial killer on the loose began to spread.

The police investigation turned up no leads, but one man knew the truth about what was happening at Briarwood Farm. He was the butcher, a twisted and deranged man who had been living in the shadows for years, silently observing the townspeople and waiting for the perfect moment to strike.

The butcher had been driven to madness by the dark energy that surrounded Briarwood Farm, and he believed that by sacrificing young women, he could appease the malevolent spirits that haunted the land. He had convinced himself that he was doing a noble deed, that his actions were necessary to save the town from a greater evil.

But when the butcher was finally caught, the town realized that the true evil had been living amongst them all along. The memory of the butcher's grisly crimes would haunt Briarwood for years to come, a reminder that even in the most idyllic of places, darkness can lurk just beneath the surface.

Chapter 45

The Lost City of the Dead

For years, archaeologist Dr. Rachel Michaels had been obsessed with the legend of the Lost City of the Dead. According to ancient texts, the city had been cursed by a powerful sorcerer, causing its inhabitants to turn into flesh-eating monsters.

Despite warnings from locals and colleagues alike, Dr. Michaels set out on an expedition to find the lost city, convinced that she could uncover its secrets and lift the curse once and for all.

As her team journeyed deep into the heart of the jungle, they encountered strange and terrifying creatures lurking in the shadows. But they pressed on, driven by their desire to uncover the truth.

Finally, after weeks of arduous travel, they stumbled upon a sprawling ruin that matched the descriptions of the Lost City of the Dead. As they entered the city, they felt an overwhelming sense of unease, as if they were being watched by unseen eyes.

The ruins were filled with grotesque depictions of human sacrifice, and the stench of decay filled the air.

But as Dr. Michaels and her team delved deeper into the city, they discovered something even more horrifying: the flesh-eating monsters of legend were real, and they were hungry.

With their backs against the wall, Dr. Michaels and her team fought for their lives, battling hordes of undead monsters that seemed impervious to injury. But even as they defeated wave after wave of the creatures, they realized that they were hopelessly outnumbered.

As the sun began to set on the city, the team made a desperate run for the exit, pursued by a relentless horde of monsters. They emerged from the ruins battered and bruised, but alive.

But as they looked back at the ruins, they knew that they had only scratched the surface of the Lost City of the Dead's secrets. The curse still hung over the city, and the monsters that lurked within were still hungry for flesh. Dr. Michaels knew that she had to warn the world of the danger that lay hidden in the jungle, before it was too late.

Chapter 46

The Phantom of the Opera House

Marie had always been fascinated by the theater, so when she landed a job as an intern at the Opera House, she was over the moon. But from the moment she stepped into the darkened halls, she felt a strange presence watching her every move.

As she worked late into the night, she began to hear whispers and footsteps coming from the empty wings of the stage. At first, she dismissed them as her imagination, but as the weeks went by, the sounds grew louder and more persistent.

One evening, Marie was practicing a solo in an empty theater when she felt a cold hand on her shoulder. She spun around to see a ghostly figure in a tattered cape and mask, its eyes burning with an otherworldly fire.

The figure introduced itself as the Phantom of the Opera House, a vengeful spirit who had been haunting the theater for centuries. It claimed to have been a failed composer who had been driven to madness by the rejection of his music, and had died in the theater in a fit of rage.

Marie tried to flee, but the Phantom was too powerful, and it dragged her back onto the stage. It demanded that she sing for it, promising to spare her life if she could please its ears.

Marie's voice rang out through the empty theater, filling the air with haunting melodies that seemed to soothe the Phantom's rage. But as the final note died away, the Phantom revealed its true intentions.

It had no intention of letting Marie go. Instead, it planned to keep her trapped in the Opera House forever, using her voice to create the haunting music it had always dreamed of.

Marie knew she had to act fast if she wanted to survive. She reached deep within herself, finding a strength and courage she had never known before. With a mighty scream, she broke free from the Phantom's grasp and raced for the exit.

As she burst through the doors, she heard the Phantom's furious cries echoing behind her. But she didn't look back. She knew that she had faced her deepest fears and triumphed over them, and she would never forget the haunting melody of the Phantom of the Opera House.

Chapter 47

The Grinning Ghost of Greenwood Cemetery

When Emma was hired to clean up the old Greenwood Cemetery, she thought it would be an easy job. But as she worked her way through the overgrown grass and crumbling headstones, she couldn't shake the feeling that she was being watched.

One night, as she was packing up her tools and getting ready to leave, she saw a figure standing in the distance. It was a ghostly apparition with a wide grin on its face, beckoning her closer.

Emma knew she should run, but she was drawn to the ghost's infectious smile. She followed the figure through the maze of graves until she came to an old mausoleum, its doors hanging open.

As she stepped inside, the doors slammed shut behind her, trapping her in the darkness. She could hear the sound of laughter echoing through the tomb, but it was not the jovial kind of laughter she had heard before.

It was the laughter of the insane, the cackling of a being that had long since lost its grip on reality.

Emma tried to escape, but the walls were too thick and the doors too heavy. She was trapped with the grinning ghost, and there was no way out.

As the ghost drew closer, its laughter growing louder and more frenzied, Emma realized that she was not dealing with a human spirit. This was something far more sinister, a demon that had taken on the guise of a friendly ghost to lure her into its clutches.

With all her strength, Emma fought back against the demonic entity, using the only weapon she had at her disposal: her own fear. She screamed and shouted, refusing to be swallowed up by the darkness.

And in the end, it was her fear that saved her. The demon recoiled at her fear, unable to withstand its power. It fled back into the shadows, leaving Emma alone in the mausoleum.

As she emerged from the tomb, shaken but alive, she knew that she had faced down one of the most terrifying creatures imaginable. And she would never forget the grinning ghost of Greenwood Cemetery, or the power of her own fear to overcome it.

Chapter 48

The Killer in the Mirror Maze

Jenny and her friends had always loved the carnival that came to town every summer. They would ride the roller coasters, play games, and indulge in all the greasy fried food they could stomach. But this year, something was different. There was a new attraction: a mirror maze.

Jenny and her friends were intrigued, and they eagerly stepped inside the maze. At first, it was fun. They laughed as they got lost and turned around, trying to find their way out. But as they went deeper into the maze, they started to notice something strange. The mirrors seemed to be distorting their reflections in unsettling ways.

Suddenly, they heard a scream. They followed the sound and found one of their friends lying on the ground, a deep gash on her neck. They tried to call for help, but their phones had no signal. They were trapped.

As they frantically tried to find their way out of the maze, they heard footsteps behind them. They turned to see a figure in a clown mask, wielding a bloody knife. They screamed and ran in the opposite direction, but they quickly realized that they were hopelessly lost.

The killer chased them through the maze, his laughter echoing off the walls. Jenny and her friends ducked into dead ends and hid behind mirrors, but the killer always seemed to find them. One by one, they fell victim to his blade.

Jenny was the only one left. She was exhausted, her heart pounding in her chest. She stumbled into a corner, trapped with the killer closing in on her. But as she looked into the mirror in front of her, she realized something shocking. The killer was not wearing a clown mask at all. It was her own reflection.

Jenny screamed as the mirror shattered, and she stumbled out of the maze, alone and terrified. She never went to a carnival again, haunted by the memory of the killer in the mirror maze.

Chapter 49

The House of the Headless Horseman

It was Halloween night when a group of teenagers decided to visit the old abandoned mansion on the edge of town. The mansion was said to be haunted by the ghost of the Headless Horseman, a ruthless warrior who had lost his head in battle and now roamed the countryside seeking revenge.

As they approached the house, they saw that the front gate was locked, so they climbed over the fence and made their way through the overgrown garden. The moon was full and bright, casting eerie shadows on the walls of the mansion.

They entered the house through a broken window and found themselves in a large foyer with a sweeping staircase. As they explored the house, they heard strange noises coming from the upper floors, and the sound of hooves on the wooden floor.

Suddenly, a gust of wind blew out all their candles, plunging the house into darkness. In the darkness, they heard the sound of a horse snorting and the clatter of hooves on the floor, growing louder and closer.

Suddenly, the Headless Horseman appeared before them, riding on a black horse with a flaming pumpkin for a head. The teenagers screamed and ran in all directions, trying to escape the wrath of the ghostly rider.

One of the teenagers, a boy named Jack, found himself trapped in a room at the end of the hallway. The door was locked and there was no escape. The Headless Horseman charged towards him, wielding a bloody axe.

But just as the Horseman was about to strike, Jack remembered something he had read about the legend of the Headless Horseman. According to the legend, if you could find the Horseman's head and return it to him, he would be able to rest in peace.

With no other options, Jack raced back through the house, dodging the Horseman's blows as he searched for the head. Finally, he found it in a hidden chamber beneath the staircase.

He returned the head to the Horseman, who let out a mournful cry before vanishing into the night. The house was still and quiet once again, and Jack was free to leave the haunted mansion.

But as he walked away from the house, he realized that he would never forget the terror of that night, and the memory of the Headless Horseman would haunt him for the rest of his days.

Chapter 50

The Secret Society of the Sorcerers

For years, rumors had circulated about a secret society of sorcerers who practiced dark magic in the shadows of the city. No one knew for sure if they truly existed, but those who claimed to have seen them spoke of unspeakable horrors and unimaginable power.

Emma had always been fascinated by the supernatural, so when she received an invitation to join the society, she couldn't resist. She was told to meet them at a secluded location in the woods outside of town, and to bring nothing but an open mind and a willingness to learn.

As she approached the meeting place, Emma felt a chill run down her spine. The air was thick with the scent of burning incense, and strange symbols were etched into the trees and rocks around her.

The sorcerers emerged from the shadows, their faces obscured by hoods and cloaks. They welcomed Emma into their midst, and began to teach her the secrets of their dark art.

At first, Emma was amazed by the things she learned. She could make objects levitate with a wave of her hand, and she could cast spells that would cause her enemies to tremble with fear. But as time went on, she began to see the true nature of the sorcerers' power.

They used their abilities for their own gain, manipulating and controlling those around them. They summoned demons and other supernatural beings to do their bidding, and reveled in the suffering and chaos they caused.

Emma knew she had made a terrible mistake by joining the society, but she was trapped. They had bound her to their will, and there seemed to be no escape.

As she delved deeper into the sorcerers' secrets, Emma realized that they were planning something truly horrifying. They were summoning a demon that would destroy the city and bring about the end of the world.

Emma knew she had to act fast to stop them. She gathered what little strength she had left and cast a spell of her own, binding the sorcerers and banishing the demon back to the underworld.

In the end, Emma knew that she had risked everything to save the world from the sorcerers' evil. But she also knew that the memory of their dark magic would haunt her for the rest of her life.

Conclusion

The Final Nightmares

As you turn the final page of "Howling Nightmares", you may find yourself looking over your shoulder, half-expecting to see a shadowy figure lurking in the darkness. The stories within these pages will linger in your mind long after you've closed the book, haunting your dreams and filling your waking hours with dread.

But as terrifying as these tales may be, they also offer a glimpse into the human psyche and the depths of our fears. Each story is a reminder that there are things in this world that we cannot fully comprehend or control, and that the darkness within us is just as dangerous as the horrors that lurk in the shadows.

Despite the terror and despair that these stories evoke, there are also moments of hope and courage. Characters who face unspeakable evil and emerge stronger for it, and who refuse to be consumed by the darkness that threatens to engulf them.

As you bid farewell to the haunted houses, cursed objects, and supernatural entities that populate these stories, know that the nightmares will continue to haunt you. But also know that you are not alone in your fear, and that there is strength to be found in confronting the unknown and standing up to the darkness.

Thank you for joining us on this journey through the world of horror, and may your nights be filled with restful slumber...if you can sleep at all.

THE End

www.ingramcontent.com/pod-product-compliance
Lightning Source LLC
Chambersburg PA
CBHW051430150726
48000CB00005B/2040